WINDOW MUSIC

PUFFIN BOOKS
Published by the Penguin Group
Penguin Putnam Books for Young Readers,
345 Hudson Street, New York, New York 10014, U.S.A.
Penguin Books Ltd, 27 Wrights Lane, London W8 5TZ, England
Penguin Books Australia Ltd, Ringwood, Victoria, Australia
Penguin Books Canada Ltd, 10 Alcorn Avenue, Toronto, Ontario, Canada M4V 3B2
Penguin Books (N.Z.) Ltd, 182-190 Wairau Road, Auckland 10, New Zealand

Penguin Books Ltd, Registered Offices: Harmondsworth, Middlesex, England

First published in the United States of America by Viking,
a member of Penguin Putnam Books for Young Readers, 1998
Published by Puffin Books, a division of Penguin Putnam Books for Young Readers, 2000

10   9   8   7   6   5   4   3   2   1

Text copyright © Anastasia Suen, 1998   Illustrations copyright © Wade Zahares, 1998
All rights reserved

THE LIBRARY OF CONGRESS HAS CATALOGED THE VIKING EDITION AS FOLLOWS:
Suen, Anastasia.
Window music/by Anastasia Suen; illustrated by Wade Zahares. p. cm.
Summary: Describes the trip taken by a train as it travels over hills, through valleys,
past horses and orange trees until it arrives at the final station.
ISBN 0-670-87287-3
[1. Railroads—Trains—Fiction. 2. Stories in rhyme.] I. Zahares, Wade, ill. II. Title.
PZ8.3.S9354Wi 1998 [E]—dc21 97-27306 CIP AC

Puffin Books ISBN 0-14-056093-9

Printed in the United States of America
Set in OptiFob

For Grandpa Maurice, Mom and Dad, and my husband Cliff . . . train lovers all. —A. S.
Thank you, Dad, for all you were, and thank you, Mom, for all you are. —W. Z.

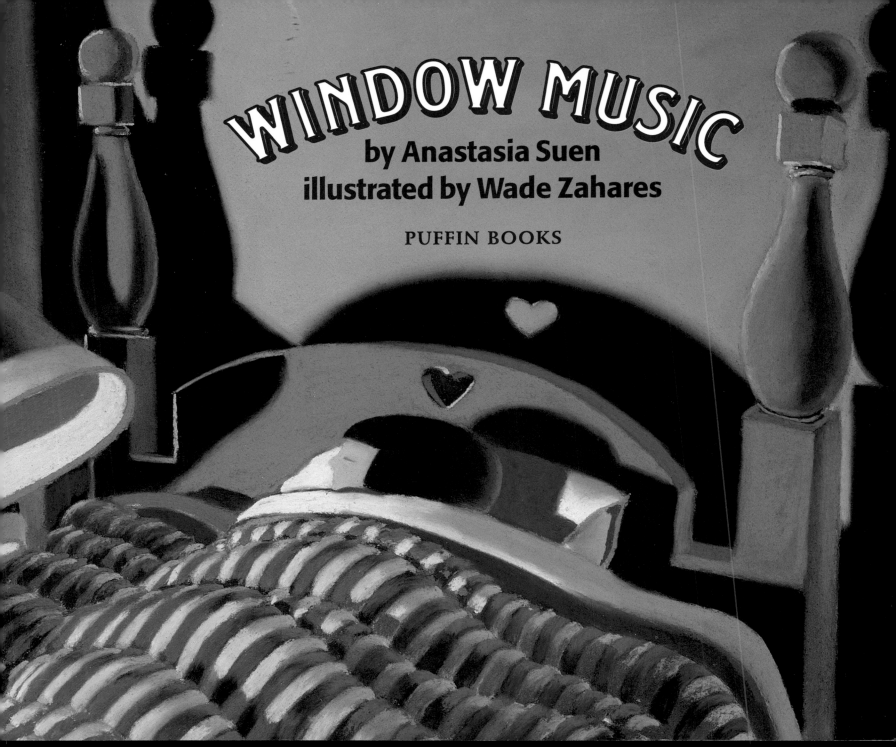

WINDOW MUSIC

by Anastasia Suen
illustrated by Wade Zahares

PUFFIN BOOKS

train on the track
clickety clack

behind the sign,
cars in line

street after street
under our feet

along the way,
horses play

in a row,
oranges grow

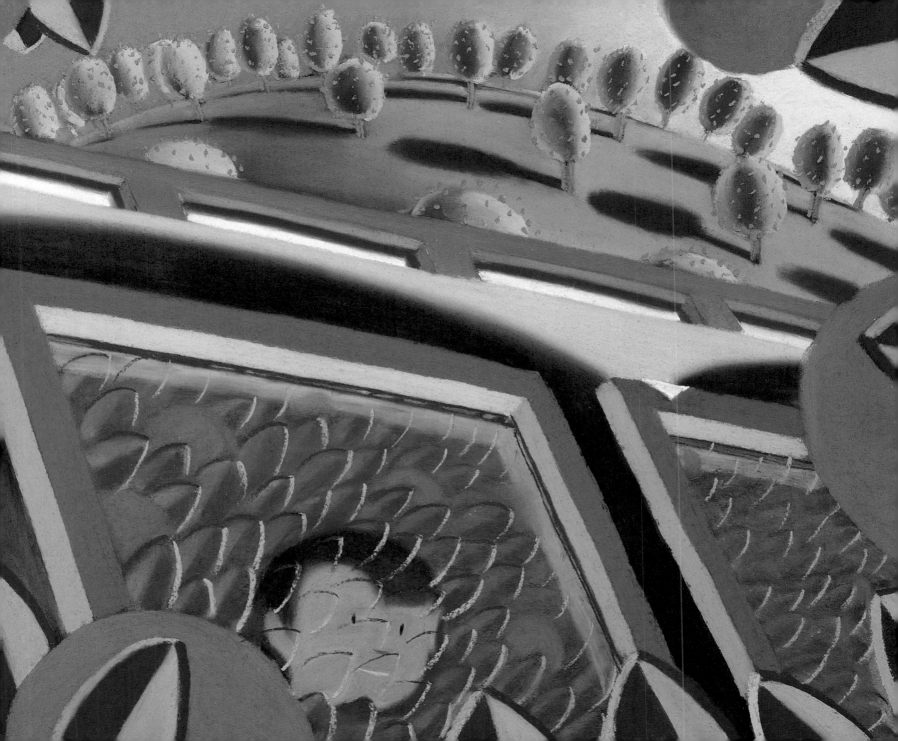

clickety clack
train on the track

waves splash,
breakers crash

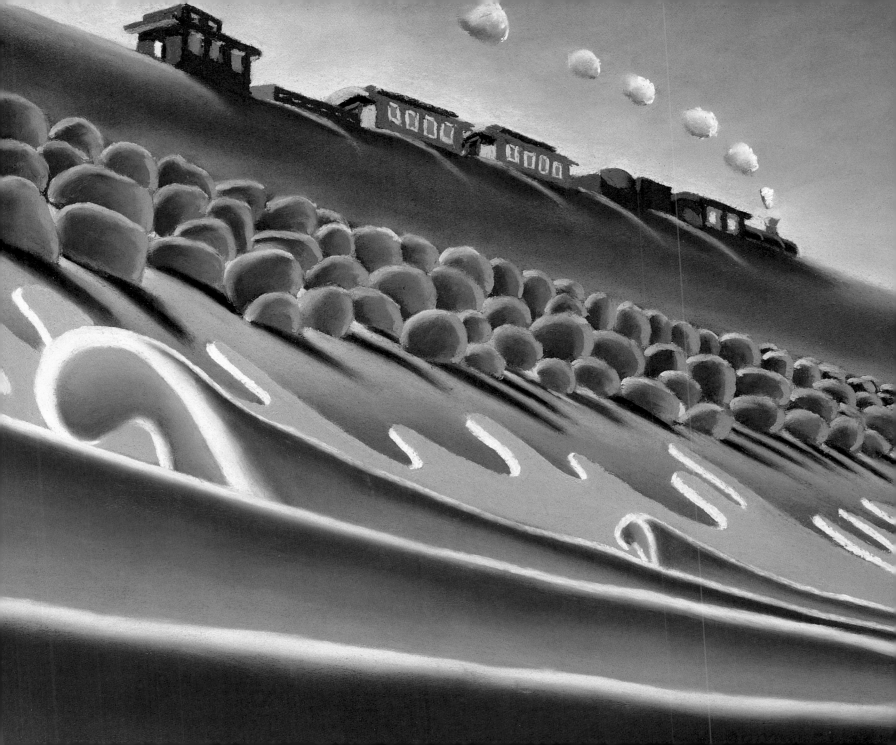

banana trees
sway in the breeze

over a hill,
grapevines spill

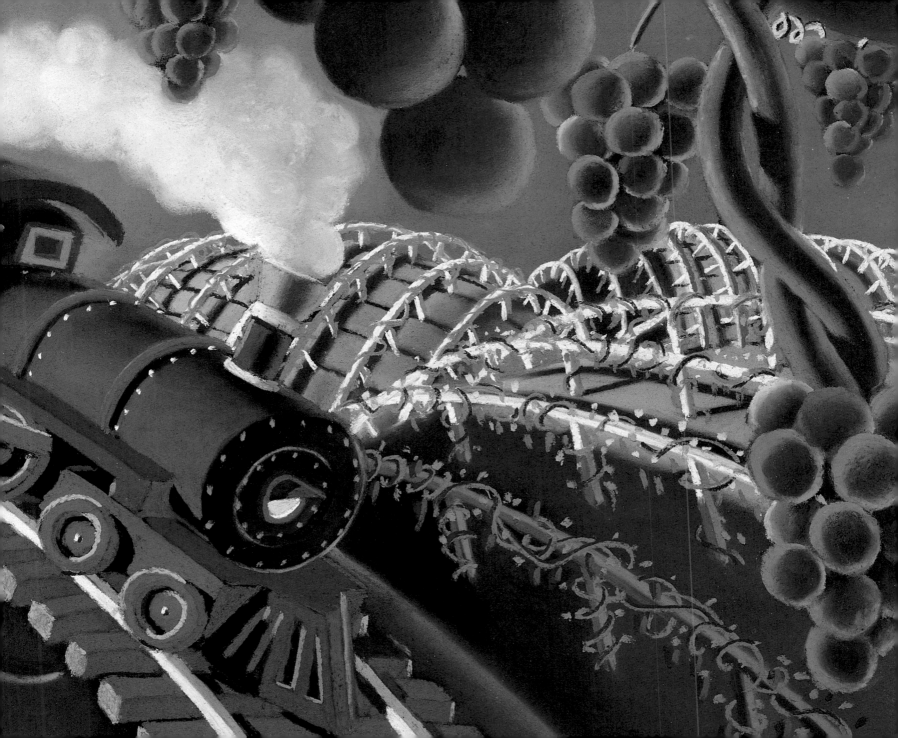

so high,
touch the sky

valley below,
down we go!

houses, streets,
the city repeats

into the station,
our destination

train on the track
clickety clack